WALT DISNEY PRODUCTIONS
presents

Goofy
and the Magic Axe

Random House   🏠   New York

Book Club Edition

First American Edition. Copyright © 1982 Walt Disney Productions. All rights reserved under International and Pan-American Copyright Conventions. Published in the United States by Random House, Inc., New York, and simultaneously in Canada by Random House of Canada Limited, Toronto. Originally published in Denmark as FEDTMULE SOM SKOVHUGGER by Gutenberghus Gruppen, Copenhagen. ISBN: 0-394-85482-9 Manufactured in the United States of America   2 3 4 5 6 7 8 9 0 A B C D E F G H I J K

Long ago there was a woodcutter
named Goofy.

He lived in a village near a forest.

Many other woodcutters lived there too.

The other woodcutters were much faster
and stronger than Goofy.

But Goofy was helpful and kind.

Everyone liked him.

One day two of the king's messengers
rode into town on their horses.

They nailed a big piece of paper
onto a tree in the town square.
It was a message from the king.

Be it known ⌒
Whoever shall cut down
the giant oak
in front of the castle
shall become the King's
Head Woodsman

⌒

The King

Everyone read the message from the king.

They all wanted to try to cut down the tree.

"I would like to try too," said Goofy.

The other woodcutters laughed and said, "Oh, Goofy, you could never do it."

So Goofy helped everyone else.
He took axes to be sharpened.
He fetched files for sharpening saws.

All the other woodcutters practiced
their chopping.
Goofy helped by bringing wood.

Finally everyone was ready
for the journey to the castle.
Goofy waved good-bye.
"Good luck," he called.

The woodcutters all had high hopes.
Each man was sure that he would
chop down the giant oak tree and
become the king's head woodsman.

A large crowd had gathered around
the oak tree in front of the castle.

There were acrobats, jugglers, and
musicians.

There was food and drink for everyone.

The woodcutters got ready
to cut down the big oak.

Men with axes
each took a turn...

and tried
to chop down
the tree.

But the tree
was so hard that
all the axes broke!

Other woodcutters used saws.

But the saws also bent and broke.
Nothing could cut the tree.

One by one the woodcutters gave up
and began the journey home.
They were very unhappy.

When the woodcutters got home,
they told Goofy what had happened.
"Gee, that's too bad," said Goofy.

"But maybe I
can try now,"
he said.

"You will never be able to chop down
that tree," said one of the woodcutters.

"How will I know if I don't try?"
said Goofy.

So Goofy went home
and got his saw...

and sharpened
his axe...

and packed
some food.

Then he set off
for the castle.

In the middle of the forest Goofy
stopped to rest and eat his food.
The forest animals gathered around him.
Friendly Goofy gave them crumbs to eat.

Along came an old man carrying
a heavy bundle of wood.
He was wearing a big floppy hat.
Goofy could hardly see his face.

The old man said, "I am so hungry and tired. Would you give me some food?"

"Of course," said Goofy. "Take all you want. I have plenty."

When the food was all gone, Goofy carried
the old man's bundle of wood home for him.
Then he stayed and chopped wood for days.
Goofy was not fast, but he worked hard.

Goofy helped in other ways too.
One day a fox scared the old man's cat.
Goofy chased the fox away.

Goofy did all he could to help the old man.
But one day he said, "I think it is time that
I left for the castle."

"I think you are right," said the old man.

"But before you go, I have a present
for you. It is a special axe. Watch!"
The old man swung the axe hard…

so that it stuck
in a tree stump.

The old man said,
"Axe, axe, do your
task!"

And the axe began
to chop all by itself.

The axe chopped
and chopped until
the whole stump
was in pieces.

"Stop, axe, stop!"
said the old man.

And the axe stopped.

"Oh, my,"
said Goofy.

So Goofy set off for the castle
with a feeling of hope.

He was sure that he could
chop down the big tree
with his magic axe.

The giant oak tree was still standing.
A few last woodcutters were just giving up.

Goofy walked up to the tree. He saw all the places where the other woodcutters had tried to chop, but he didn't lose hope.

He wasn't even nervous when the king came out of the castle to watch him.

Goofy lifted the axe.
The old man had told
him to hold on tight,
so Goofy did.
Then he said, "Axe,
axe, do your task!"

Sure enough, the axe began to chop
all by itself.

It bit right into the hard wood.

Goofy held on for his life!

When the tree was ready to fall,
Goofy shouted, "Stop, axe, stop!"
The axe stopped chopping, and
the tree fell with a crash.

"Well done!"
said the king.

The king took Goofy
into the castle.

"You are the best woodcutter
in the land," said the king.

"And now, Goofy, you will be rewarded."

"Thank you," said Goofy, "but first
I must go and thank the old man who
gave me this wonderful axe."

"There is no need to do that,"
said the king.

He threw off his royal robes.
"I am that old man you met
in the forest," said the king.

"I gave you the magic axe because
you were kind to me."
Goofy was very happy to see
his friend—and his friend's cat!

"You will be my head woodsman,"
said the king. "I was looking for
someone just like you."

"You help other people and you share
what you have. You are kind and honest.
You are just the sort of woodsman that
I want."

So Goofy became the king's head woodsman.
He took care of all the forests and
the forest animals.
    And he spent many happy days in the castle
with the king and his cat.